This book belongs to:

_____

For Farmer George and all the other farmers too,
and everyone who likes to go... BOO! – S.W.

For Olive, the Friesian Greyhound – F.B.

First published in Great Britain in 2021 by Andersen Press Ltd., 20 Vauxhall Bridge Road, London SW1V 2SA.

Text copyright © Steve Webb 2021. Illustration copyright © Fred Blunt 2021.

The rights of Steve Webb and Fred Blunt to be identified as the author and illustrator of this work have been asserted by

them in accordance with the Copyright, Designs and Patents Act, 1988. All rights reserved. Printed and bound in China.

1 3 5 7 9 10 8 6 4 2

British Library Cataloguing in Publication Data available.

Hardback ISBN 978 1 83913 022 9
Paperback ISBN 978 1 83913 023 6

COWS GO BOO!

Steve Webb

Fred Blunt

Andersen Press

On Farmer George's farm the pigs go...

Oink!

The sheep go...

Baaa!

And the COWS go...

where did all the cows go?

Farmer George got such a fright,
he jumped out of his wellies.

NO, NO, NO! Pigs go oink, sheep go baa, but cows do not go BOO. Cows go MOO! Please try to get it right.

On Farmer George's farm the truck goes...

Beep!

The tractor goes...

Vroom!

And the cows go... where did all the cows go?

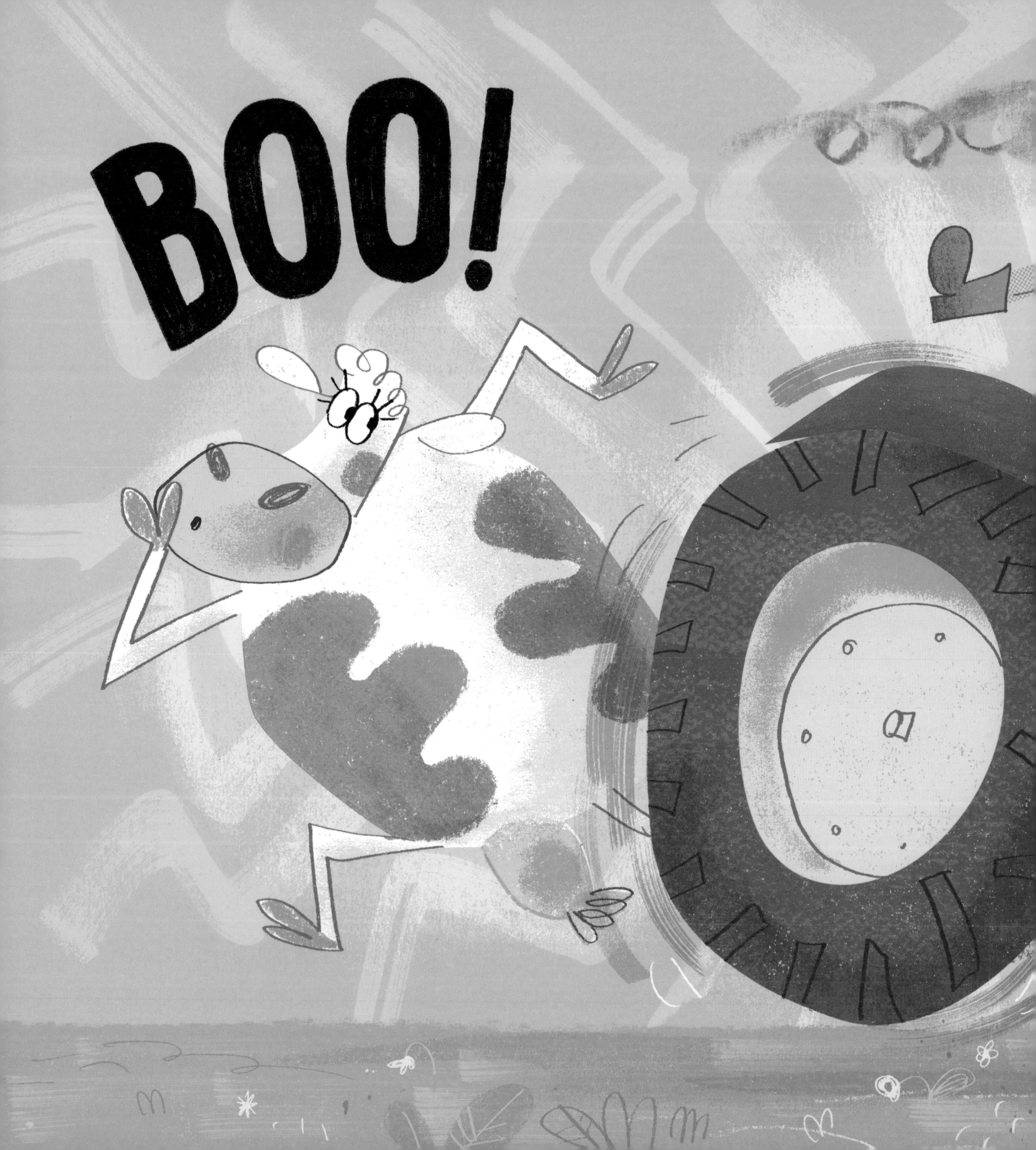
BOO!

In Farmer George's farmhouse the dog goes

Woof!

The cat goes

Meow!

Farmer George got such a fright he spilled his cup of tea all over the sofa.

Farmer George was cleaning up the mess when he had the most **fabulous** idea.

Come with me, **cows** that go **BOO**.

He led the cows up to the top field, where
the scarecrow was not doing a very good job of
scaring away the birds from his crops.

In Farmer George's scarecrow field the cows go...
where did all the cows go?